ready, steady, read!

The Get-away Hen

Martin Waddell
Illustrated by Susie Jenkin-Pearce

Puffin Books

For the brave hen Crusty and her friends   S. J.-P.

PUFFIN BOOKS

Published by the Penguin Group
Penguin Books Ltd, 27 Wrights Lane, London W8 5TZ, England
Penguin Books USA Inc., 375 Hudson Street, New York, NY 10014, USA
Penguin Books Australia Ltd, Ringwood, Victoria, Australia
Penguin Books Canada Ltd, 10 Alcorn Avenue, Toronto, Ontario, Canada M4V 3B2
Penguin Books (NZ) Ltd, 182–190 Wairau Road, Auckland 10, New Zealand

Penguin Books Ltd, Registered Offices: Harmondsworth, Middlesex, England

Published in Puffin Books 1993
10 9 8 7 6 5 4 3 2

Filmset in Monotype Bembo Schoolbook

Printed in England by Clays Ltd, St Ives plc

Brown Hen lived in a cage in a
house full of hens.

She sat in dim light and warm air, and soft music played, but she never saw night or the light of the stars. All she could see was the roof of the house, which was painted a dull shade of yellow.

She was fed by a machine
tipping her food out into a tray.
She could eat without stretching
her neck.

"Thanks very much!" thought Brown Hen (though she didn't know who to thank). She pecked the food up, and then she laid an egg. The egg rolled away down a chute, and she never saw it again.

Brown Hen was bored and she started complaining.

"Is this it?" she asked. "Is this all that there is to my life?"

8

"Maybe it is," said the others.
"But you're well fed and warm, so
shut up!"

"I want to find out what my
life is about!" said Brown Hen,
and she sat in her cage and
dreamed of *something*. She didn't
quite know what it was.

Then one night things went
wrong. Someone pulled a switch
by mistake and . . .

. . . the lights flickered out and the warm air turned cold. The soft music stopped and the doors of the cages popped wide open.

The hens were all scared. They started to squawk at their trays, hoping food would come out as it usually did, but it didn't.

"What's this all about?" Brown Hen asked the others. They huddled up to the bars of their cages and shivered with shock.

"It's about being afraid!" said the hens, because that's what they felt, now that their house was all dark and cold.

"I'm not afraid," said Brown Hen.

"We are!" squawked the other hens.

"Well, I'm off," said Brown Hen, plopping down from her cage on to the floor.

"Don't go!" squawked the other hens, but Brown Hen didn't listen.

She'd never moved much,
penned up in her cage, so her legs
didn't work very well, but she
managed a flutter. She got up on
to her feet and she wobbled about.

Brown Hen saw a bright light . . .

. . . and she wobbled towards it . . .

. . . and she wobbled OUT.

"Oh my!" gasped Brown Hen.
She gazed in delight at the
moon. It was big and bright
and lit up the night.

"I should be scared, but
I'm not," thought Brown
Hen. "Look at me, all
alone in a world with
no roof."

RRRRRRRRRRRRRRRRR!

Something ran into the yard.

Brown Hen didn't wait to find out

what it was. (It was a dog.)

She flapped her wings and she
ran (though she didn't know she
could run) and escaped.

"What's this all about?" panted Brown Hen. She could have stayed where she was, but she didn't. She was excited. She wanted to see more of the world with no roof. She thought she might like it.

GRRRRRRRRRRRRRRRR!

Brown Hen saw bright eyes and sharp teeth!

Brown Hen guessed the thing might eat her (though she didn't know what a fox was), so she squawked . . .

. . . and she fluttered . . .

. . . and ran . . .

. . . and she hid high in the hedge,
where the fox couldn't eat her.

"Oh my!" gasped Brown Hen.
"I nearly got eaten!"

She sat all alone, counting the feathers she'd lost, waiting for food to pop out of the hedge on a tray. But no food came out.

Brown Hen went to sleep in the
hedge, feeling hungry.

Brown Hen slept until dawn
and then she woke up.

"Oh my!" gasped Brown Hen. She saw the sunlight for the very first time and she liked it a lot (though she didn't know what the sun was).

The light was so bright that it dazzled Brown Hen. She tucked her head under her wing, shielding her eyes.

COCK-A-DOODLE-DOO!
COCK-A-DOODLE-DOO!

Brown Hen forgot all her fear of the dog and the fox and the sun, and ran over the fields. She wanted to see who was making the noise.

It was a cock, puffing his chest
and crowing for all he was worth.
The cock looked a bit like a hen,
which made her feel safer,
somehow.

"Why hello there, little hen,"
the cock said, turning his head.
"You're new around here. I've not
seen you before."

"That's right," said Brown Hen.
"I lived over there, but I'm not
going back, because
I like it here."

"I'll show you around," said the cock, and he marched Brown Hen about as though he owned the place, though he didn't.

There wasn't a house full of hens and music and warm lights, or a tray of food, but there was a yard full of hens all pecking the ground.

They clucked and gossiped a lot
with their friends, not like the hens
that she'd left in the house.

"What's this all about?" asked
Brown Hen.

"We're finding our food!" said
the hens.

"On the ground?" gasped
Brown Hen, feeling slightly
disgusted.

"Where else?" said the hens.
"Why don't you try it and see?"

Brown Hen pecked a bit on her own (once she'd worked out what to peck for). The food on the ground didn't look like the food that she used to find in her tray, but it tasted much better, although some of it wriggled about.

Then it was time for her egg, so she laid it. She sat and she waited for her egg to roll down the chute, but there was no chute, so the egg didn't roll; it stayed where it was.

Brown Hen looked at the egg,
the very first egg that she'd laid
which had stayed, without rolling
off down the chute.

"What's this all about?" Brown Hen asked the cock.

"Sit on it and see!" said the cock, with his head on one side.

"How long for?" asked Brown Hen.

"For as long as it takes!" said
the cock, strutting off.

"I don't think my life is about
sitting on top of an egg!" grumbled
Brown Hen, but she sat on her egg
to see what would happen.

Brown Hen sat a long time all alone. She felt a bit silly, sitting alone on an egg.

She sat . . .

. . . and she sat . . .

. . . and she sat . . .

. . . and then something stirred in the egg, hidden warm underneath her.

"Oh my!" gasped Brown Hen.

The egg started jigging about. Brown Hen got up on her feet, feeling puzzled. She'd seen eggs that rolled, but she'd never seen an egg jig (and she didn't know what was making it jig).

And then . . .

. . . the egg broke . . .

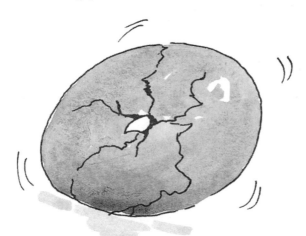

. . . and a small beak appeared,
pecking its way out of the egg.

"Oh my!" gasped Brown Hen, and she called to the cock. "What's this all about?"

"Don't ask me!" said the cock. "It just happens!" (He'd seen it happen before.)

And then . . .

. . . *something* wet and small clambered out through the roof of the egg, and snuggled up close to Brown Hen.

"What's *this*?" asked Brown
Hen, looking down at the small
beaky face just below her.

"It's your chick," said the cock,
preening himself.

Brown Hen looked at her chick, and something stirred in her hen-heart. She gave him a peck (very gently) then she pushed him about, till the very small chick stood up on his very small feet.

He took three trembly steps, and then he fell down on his very small bottom.

"Oh my!" said the chick.

The world looked scary and big to the chick, and he hid his head under his wing.

"Don't be scared, little chick,"
said Brown Hen. "You're small
and I'm big, but I'll look after you
until you are bigger."

The chick raised his head from under his wing. "This world's not like the world in my egg," said the chick. "This world has no roof."

"Who needs a roof?" said
Brown Hen.

She'd found out what living was
for . . .

Brown Hen wasn't alone
any more.

ready, steady, read!

Other books in this series